D0394321

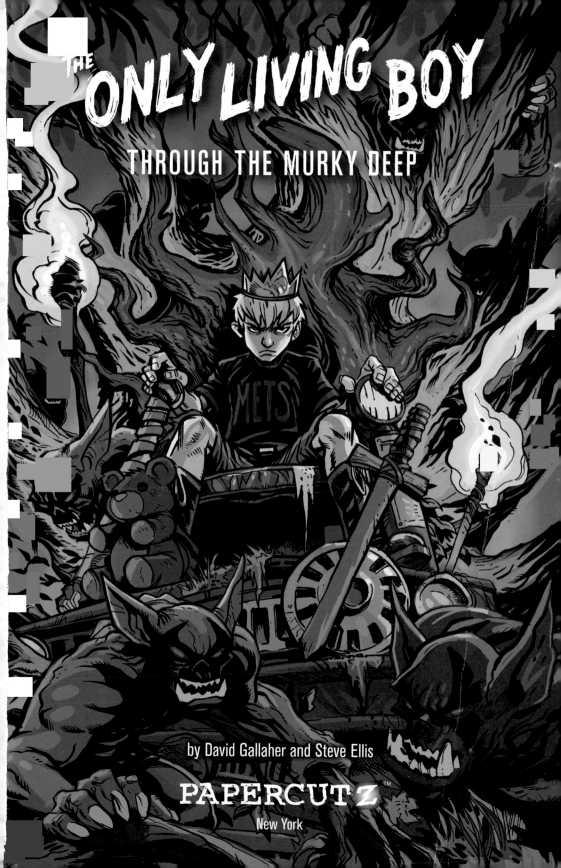

To Drew, Ben and Daniel for being the
greatest brothers – David

To Jacob and Luna and to exploring life's
greatest adventures – Steve

THE ONLY LIVING BOY #4 "Through the Murky Deep"

Chapters 7 & 8
Writer / Co-Creator: David Gallaher
Artist / Co-Creator: Steve Ellis
Color Flatting: Holley McKend
Lettering: Melanie Ujimori
Consulting Editor: Janelle Asselin
Production Assistance: Allison Strejlau
Assistants: Emily Walton, Luke D. Blackwood

Special Thanks to Dara Hyde

Originally serialized at: www.the-only-living-boy.com

Papercutz books may be purchased for business or promotional use.
For information on bulk purchases please contact Macmillan Corporate and
Premium Sales Department at
(800) 221-795 x5442.

Production – Dawn Guzzo
Cover Logo – Adam Grano
Production Coordinator – Sasha Kimiatek
Assistant Managing Editor - Jeff Whitman
Jim Salicrup
Editor-in-Chief

PB ISBN: 978-1-62991-634-7
HC ISBN: 978-1-62991-635-4

Printed in China. April 2017

Distributed by Macmillan
First Papercutz Printing

CHAPTER SEVEN

Previously in...

THE ONLY LIVING BOY

After an epic battle at the Hive City of Sectuarius, Erik finds himself at the mercy of Doctor Once and Baalikar. While captured, Erik learns that the creatures he freed from the Census have all been re-captured and subjected to horrible experiments. When he tries to confront Doctor Once, Erik soon finds himself the victim of cruel experiments that reveal his tragic past of loss, loneliness, and death. After fighting back, Erik was able to force Doctor Once to reveal his own path of heartbreak that led the fiendish scientist to create Baalikar and the Patchwork Planet. Fatally wounded from his own machines, with his dying breath, Doctor Once begs Erik to travel North, far beyond the reach of Baalikar's watch. After freeing the rest of the creatures, Erik runs into the woods seeking shelter, where he finds a handmade doll made by the savage Alku. Raising the doll to the sky in a fit of rage, Erik may have just gotten more than he bargained for.

I DON'T UNDERSTAND. I'M PRETTY SURE YOU GUYS TRIED TO EAT ME WHEN I FIRST ARRIVED HERE.

ALKU!

ALKU!

BUT MAYBE YOU WERE TRYING TO DEFEND YOUR HOME?

THAT'S US, BEAR.

AND THAT'S WHEN WE FIRST ENCOUNTERED MORGAN.

AND THE ROZAK.

ALKU! ALKU!

AND THE DOLL YOU MADE OF ME.

ALKU!

OKAY... BUT WHY ARE THEY ALL ABOUT ME?

I MEAN... YOU'RE TELLING STORIES ABOUT ME...

...AND CARVING UP TREES TO DO IT. IT'S VERY FLATTERING, BUT--

ALKU!

I THINK I HAVE TO DO THIS ALONE, KLEEF.

I CAN'T RISK PUTTING ANY OF YOU IN DANGER. I JUST--

≶sigh≷

SOME CHALLENGES WE MUST FACE ALONE, OUTLANDER. I UNDERSTAND.

...BUT THERE IS NO NEED FOR TEARS.

AFTER I WAS CAPTURED, I WAS CERTAIN THAT I WOULD MEET THE CRUELEST OF ENDS.

YOU CHANGED ALL OF THAT.

WHEN YOU MARCH THROUGH THAT WASTE SWAMP, I WANT YOU TO REMEMBER THIS.

...YOU SHOULDN'T FEAR THE UNKNOWN, THE UNKNOWN SHOULD FEAR YOU.

WELL, WHEN YOU PUT IT THAT WAY...

I'M GOING TO GET MY SWORD.

28

CHAPTER EIGHT

I CAN'T REALLY SEE.

RELAX, HUMAN.

OUR BODIES HAVE ADAPTED TO HELP US NAVIGATE THE UNUSUAL CLIMATES OF THIS WORLD. OBSERVE.

THE GROUNDLINGS WERE AMONG OUR FIRST ALLIES.

AFTER THE LANDGRAF FELL INTO RUIN, THEY BECAME OUR ONLY ALLIES.

AND EVEN *THAT* RELATIONSHIP IS STRAINED.

THERE'S PLENTY OF TIME TO CHANGE THAT.

WATCH OUT FOR PAPERCUTZ™

Welcome to the fear-fraught fourth THE ONLY LIVING BOY graphic novel, by David Gallaher and Steve Ellis, from Papercutz – those patchwork people dedicated to publishing great graphic novels for all ages. I'm Jim Salicrup, Editor-in-Chief and the only living fanboy working at 160 Broadway on wintery weekends, here to offer up a poem...

Yes, I said "a poem"! I know I usually use my "My Watch Out for Papercutz" column to bring you up-to-date on the latest Papercutz news, but you can always check out papercutz.com for that. I'm resorting to publishing poetry because of Erik Farrell's current dire situation. I mean, after what's happened to the poor kid in THE ONLY LIVING BOY #3, I would totally understand if he just wanted to find a bed to hide in under the blankets for a year or so. Not that that would've made an especially exciting graphic novel! But Erik is something special. Like the watches in the long ago advertising slogan for Timex, Erik can take a beating and keep on ticking.

I know none any of us have been in exactly the predicament Erik's in now, but I'm sure we've all had to deal with major problems at some point. Who hasn't ever felt lost? Or felt that everything wasn't going your way? I think we all do at various times, especially when we've had to deal with seriously unpleasant things. I deal with it by trying to embrace all the positive things in my life–family, friends, comics, music, movies, etc. – and to remember this corny old poem by Frank Lebby Stanton (1857-1927) that I'd like to share with you now. It's called...

Keep A-Goin'
by Frank L. Stanton

If you strike a thorn or rose,
Keep a-goin'!
If it hails or if it snows,
Keep a-goin'!
'Taint no use to sit an' whine
When the fish ain't on your line;
Bait your hook an' keep a-tryin'--
Keep a goin'!

When the weather kills your crop,
Keep a-goin'!
Though 'tis work to reach the top,
Keep a-goin'!
S'pose you're out o' ev'ry dime,
Gittin' broke ain't any crime;
Tell the world you're feelin' prime--
Keep a-goin'!

When it looks like all is up,
Keep a-goin'!
Drain the sweetness from the cup,
Keep a-goin'!
See the wild birds on the wing,
Hear the bells that sweetly ring,
When you feel like singin', sing--
Keep a-goin'!

And that's what Erik does in this graphic novel, and that reminds me of the adage, "Be careful what you wish for..." because in THE ONLY LIVING BOY #5, Erik's confrontation with the mind-boggling, super-powerful Baalikar continues, and we can only hope that the only living boy can continue to keep on living! Be there for "To Save a Shattered World," Erik can use all the support he can get!

Thanks, and keep a-goin',

STAY IN TOUCH!

EMAIL: salicrup@papercutz.com
WEB: papercutz.com
TWITTER: @papercutzgn
FACEBOOK: PAPERCUTZGRAPHICNOVELS
FAN MAIL: Papercutz, 160 Broadway, Suite 700, East Wing, New York, NY 10038